The Trouble with Grandad

To my gardener

The Trouble with Grandad

Babette Cole

MAMMOTH

The trouble with Grandad is . . .

he grows such enormous vegetables.

They won all the prizes
at the Vegetable Show.

The other exhibitors were very jealous.
"We'll fix him!" they said.

So one of them gave him
a funny looking tomato plant.

It grew quite big.

Then bigger . . .

and bigger,

until it was taller
than the local
police station.

Grandad was arrested for
growing a dangerous vegetable!

The police asked the fire brigade to spray
Grandad's tomato with weed killer . . .

and the army to blow it up . . .

and the Secret Service
to destroy it
with a secret
weapon.

But it just kept growing. So they let Grandad
out to see if he could stop it.

"It's got worms!" said Grandad.

Sure enough, out popped
an enormous caterpillar.

It ate and ate until the tomato had gone.

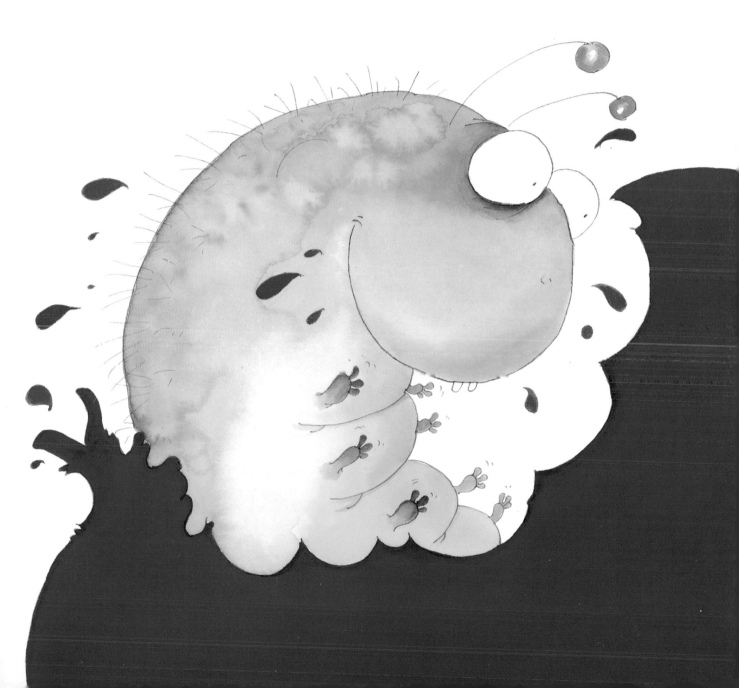

Then it went to sleep.

That night

the prisoners
broke out of
their cells.

But they soon ran back inside again!

The caterpillar turned into a chrysalis.

The police station couldn't take the strain!

The police were furious with Grandad.

Luckily, the chrysalis turned into
a huge moth just in time.

Back at the allotment Grandad hollowed out
his biggest ever cucumber . . .

The police are very happy
with their new station.

But they have to watch out
for the slugs!

First published in Great Britain 1988
by William Heinemann Ltd
This edition published 1989
by Mammoth
an imprint of Reed Consumer Books Ltd
Michelin House, 81 Fulham Road, London SW3 6RB
and Auckland, Melbourne, Singapore and Toronto

Reprinted 1989, 1991 (twice), 1992, 1993, 1994, 1996

Produced by Mandarin Offset Ltd
Printed and bound in Hong Kong

ISBN 0 7497 0022 X